Who's Your Candidate? Choosing Government Leaders

Becoming a SENATOR

By Maria Nelson

Gareth Stevens PUBLISHING

Please visit our website, www.garethstevens.com. For a free color catalog of all our high-quality books, call toll free 1-800-542-2595 or fax 1-877-542-2596.

Cataloging-in-Publication Data

Nelson, Maria.
Becoming a senator / by Maria Nelson.
p. cm. — (Who's your candidate? Choosing government leaders)
Includes index.
ISBN 978-1-4824-4043-0 (pbk.)
ISBN 978-1-4824-4044-7 (6-pack)
ISBN 978-1-4824-4045-4 (library binding)
1. Legislators — United States — Juvenile literature. 2. United States. — Congress. — Senate — Juvenile literature. 3. United States — Politics and government — Juvenile literature. I. Nelson, Maria. II. Title.
JK1276.N45 2016
328.73—d23

Published in 2016 by
Gareth Stevens Publishing
111 East 14th Street, Suite 349
New York, NY 10003

Designer: Andrea Davison-Bartolotta
Editor: Kristen Nelson

Photo credits: Cover, p. 1 Jupiterimages/Getty Images; cover, p. 1 Cvandyke/Shutterstock.com; p. 4 holbox/Shutterstock.com; p. 5 Jupiterimages/Photos.com/Thinkstock; pp. 6–7 Melina Mera/The Washington Post/Getty Images; p. 9 Jupiterimages/Stockbyte/Thinkstock; pp. 10–11 Senate Photo Studio/Wikimedia Commons; p. 12 (website) courtesy of www.gillibrand.senate.gov; pp. 12–13 (computer) Nattstudio/Shutterstock.com; p. 13 Alistair Berg/Getty Images; p. 14 Jessica McGowan/Getty Images; p. 15 Mark Bowden/iStock/Thinkstock; p. 17 Bill Clark/CQ Roll Call/Getty Images; p. 18 Scott J. Ferrell/Congressional Quarterly/Getty Images; p. 19 (main) Mark Wilson/Getty Images; p. 19 (inset) Mladen Antonov/AFP/Getty Images; pp. 20–21 Amir Ridhwan/Shutterstock.com; p. 23 Spencer Platt/Getty Images; pp. 24–25 Alex Wong/Getty Images; p. 27 Tom Williams/CQ Roll Call/Getty Images; p. 28 Andrew Harrer/Bloomberg/Getty Images; pp. 28–29 AVAVA/Shutterstock.com.

Printed in the United States of America

CPSIA compliance information: Batch #CW16GS: For further information contact Gareth Stevens, New York, New York at 1-800-542-2595.

CONTENTS

Words in the glossary appear in **bold** type the first time they are used in the text.

The Next Step

Have you been a team captain for a few years? Or maybe you've been a club president or a homeroom leader. Once you have taken on a few small student leadership positions, you might feel ready to run for a position in a school-wide group, such as student council.

Candidates for the US Senate are often in a similar situation! They may have been a governor or served a few terms as a congressperson in the House of Representatives. They're ready to take a chance in a statewide election and possibly gain a seat in the Senate.

The Higher House

The Senate is one of the two houses of Congress, the legislative—or lawmaking—body of the US government. There are 100 senators in office at any time. Each state is equally represented in the Senate with two senators. In the House of Representatives, a state's representation is based on its population.

US Capitol

Just as senators represent their state in the federal government, you could represent your class or school!

Deciding to run for Senate or student council is a big decision! Each takes up a lot of time, both campaigning and the duties of the job. Candidates need to make sure they're ready for it! Then, they should make sure they're qualified to run.

Candidates for the House of Representatives must be at least 25 years old and citizens for 7 years. The Founding Fathers wanted senators to be a little older and wiser than representatives.

According to the US Constitution, candidates for the US Senate must be at least 30 years old. They have to live in the state they'd like to represent. Senators have to be a US citizen for at least 9 years before running. That means senators don't have to be born in the United States. They can be **naturalized** citizens!

Your Turn!

If you like to make decisions and be in charge, running for a student leadership position is a great way to use your skills! Many schools have student councils that speak on behalf of students and plan events. Your class or homeroom might also have a group that leads it. You could also start your own **volunteer** group or club and lead it from the beginning!

Common Backgrounds

Before running for Senate, candidates can have just about any job. Some backgrounds are more common than others. Of senators in office in 2014, more than half were lawyers or had a law degree. Jobs in business or as a local or state-level official are also usual for senators. Teachers or others who worked in education often run for Senate, too. Farmers, doctors, and military officers have also been senators in the past.

What's more important than what kind of job candidates had are the skills they learned at it. Similarly, your experiences before running for a student leadership position can make you a better candidate.

Senate Appointment

Not all senators are elected to their office. When a senator dies or can't finish his or her term, the state's governor commonly appoints someone to fill that seat in the Senate. This person may serve until the end of the senator's term or until a special election can be held, depending on the state. Some states don't appoint anyone and hold special elections as soon as possible.

Being a club president gave you a chance to lead others. Performing in a school play taught you how to speak in front of many people. Let voters know you have these skills!

Term Talk

Senators serve for 6 years at a time, but House representatives only serve 2-year terms. The term lengths were choices of the Founding Fathers, too. A 6-year term allows senators to work on their **agenda** for a longer period of time and consider the long-term effects of the government's actions. While House representatives are very connected to their **constituency**, senators are supposed to be more independent of what the public thinks. In this way, the two houses of Congress balance one another.

Every 2 years, one-third of the Senate is up for reelection. This way, most senators are focused on what's happening in Congress rather than campaigning most of the time.

Politics, Parties, and Primaries

The US government generally has a two-party system. Most politicians identify as either a Democrat or Republican. Before running for Senate, candidates have to win their party's **primary**. If they win, they run against the other party's candidate. Would-be senators have to campaign for primary elections, too!

The room, or chamber, the Senate works in is in the Capitol building in the US capital city of Washington, DC.

The Campaign Trail

Choosing to run for Senate will not only be tiring, but also costly. Some candidates use their own money to run their campaign, especially to start. Most candidates need money from donors. They have to attend parties to meet people who might want to give money to the campaign and often travel all around their home state. Once a candidate raises or spends $5,000 on the campaign, he or she has to officially register as a candidate.

Campaign money is used to help get a candidate's name out to voters. Posters, buttons, and TV commercials are just some of the ways to advertise a candidacy.

Your Turn!

Student leaders can make a big difference at a school. You might be able to introduce ideas from the students' view that a teacher or the principal didn't think of! If you have a big idea—like a school-wide volunteering day or a change to the school lunch policy—make sure you'll be allowed to do it if you're elected. Then, be sure to let the voters know your message!

Twitter, Facebook, and other social media are a great way for you and federal politicians to reach voters! Having a website just for your campaign is a useful idea, too.

The main reason candidates for Senate need to campaign is to let voters know what they're going to do if elected. This message often has certain promises and goals especially for the state, such as gaining more federal money to fix roads or support farmers. Candidates often try to meet members of their constituency and answer their questions. It's important to get this message to voters because they elect senators directly! One person's vote can mean a lot in a Senate election.

Once elected, senators have to take an oath of office. Senators promise to support the US Constitution.

Your Turn!

Perhaps the best way to get votes when running for student council or other school leadership is by getting involved. Attend sports games and band concerts, and help a club with their bake sale. The more people who know your name and face, the better your chances of being elected!

Senator David Perdue campaigning in 2014

Taking part in school and community activities is a great way to meet people and show your support for others.

Job Description

Once elected, a senator has a very important job! Senators are directly involved in making laws that affect US citizens. This includes talking to **lobbyists** and doing research about many topics. They may take part in writing laws and presenting them to other members of Congress, too. Sometimes, senators get to work with the president on laws he or she wants to pass!

Senators must have knowledge about a lot of different topics, from the military to the federal budget. In order to make informed decisions when voting on bills, they must be willing to continue learning about these topics throughout their term.

Stamp of Approval

In addition to making laws, the Senate makes the final decision about many government appointments. It takes a majority in the Senate to approve Supreme Court justices, ambassadors, and the president's closest advisors, the Cabinet. The Senate also ratifies, or approves, treaties, but two-thirds of senators have to agree.

Senators have a staff to help them get everything done. There are people in charge of the campaign, money, travel plans, and more.

Senator Rand Paul

Senators split their time between working in Washington, DC, when Congress is in session and their home state. When in their state, senators travel to many cities and areas to find out constituents' concerns. While House representatives are more bound by voters' wants, senators also work to represent their state's needs.

In both places, senators' days are busy. Whether they're meeting with their committee, staff, or constituents, senators spend a lot of time with other people. Before a congressional session ends, it commonly gets even busier as people want certain issues brought up and bills passed. Senators may not see their family much during this time!

The Committee System

How does the Senate deal with all the decisions it must make and bills that are submitted to it? Every senator is a member of at least one committee. These smaller groups take on a certain area, such as foreign relations or finance, and learn as much as they can about it. Committees then advise the rest of the Senate about a subject.

Senate committee meeting

Even though a vote in the Senate only takes a few minutes, the **debate** about a bill or topic can go on for a long time. Sometimes, a senator will try to stop a vote on a bill by speaking for a long time. This is called a filibuster. In 2013, Senator Ted Cruz spoke for 21 hours straight!

You, in Office!

Just like a senator, a student leader spends a lot of time campaigning. Then, leading up to election day, you might have to give a speech or take part in a debate with your opponents. Planning for these events takes a lot of effort, but the election will be over before you know it!

While student council members may not have a staff like a senator does, having people around to help you plan and organize events is a great way to make sure items on your agenda get done well.

As your campaign wraps up, start thinking about what you'll do once elected.

- Thank all your voters on your campaign's social media accounts.
- Get to know others you'll be working with, including teachers.
- Have a list of actions you'd like to take and how to start working on them.
- Start gathering classmates, teammates, and friends to help you lead.

Your Turn!

If you made any campaign promises, you should have explored a plan of action to enact them. This includes talking to the school **administrators** about whether there's enough money for it or brainstorming with your friends about the best way to get others to take part in your idea. However you plan it out, make sure to keep your promises!

Seniority

Simply becoming a senator doesn't immediately earn you respect in the Senate. In fact, some senators have a hard time getting much done for their state during their first term! That's because the Senate greatly values **seniority**. Some senators are in office for so long that someone who has served just one or two terms seems inexperienced!

First-time senators who've worked their way up through lower offices, such as mayor, member of a state **legislature**, or the House of Representatives have an easier time being accepted than those of other backgrounds. Senators slowly gain **influence** by working hard, learning from others, and showing trustworthiness.

Your Turn!

Seniority often plays a part in student leadership, too. If you want to be student council president someday, consider running for a lower office such as secretary or class representative. Like a new senator, you can show others how good you'd be for a future position by doing another one well!

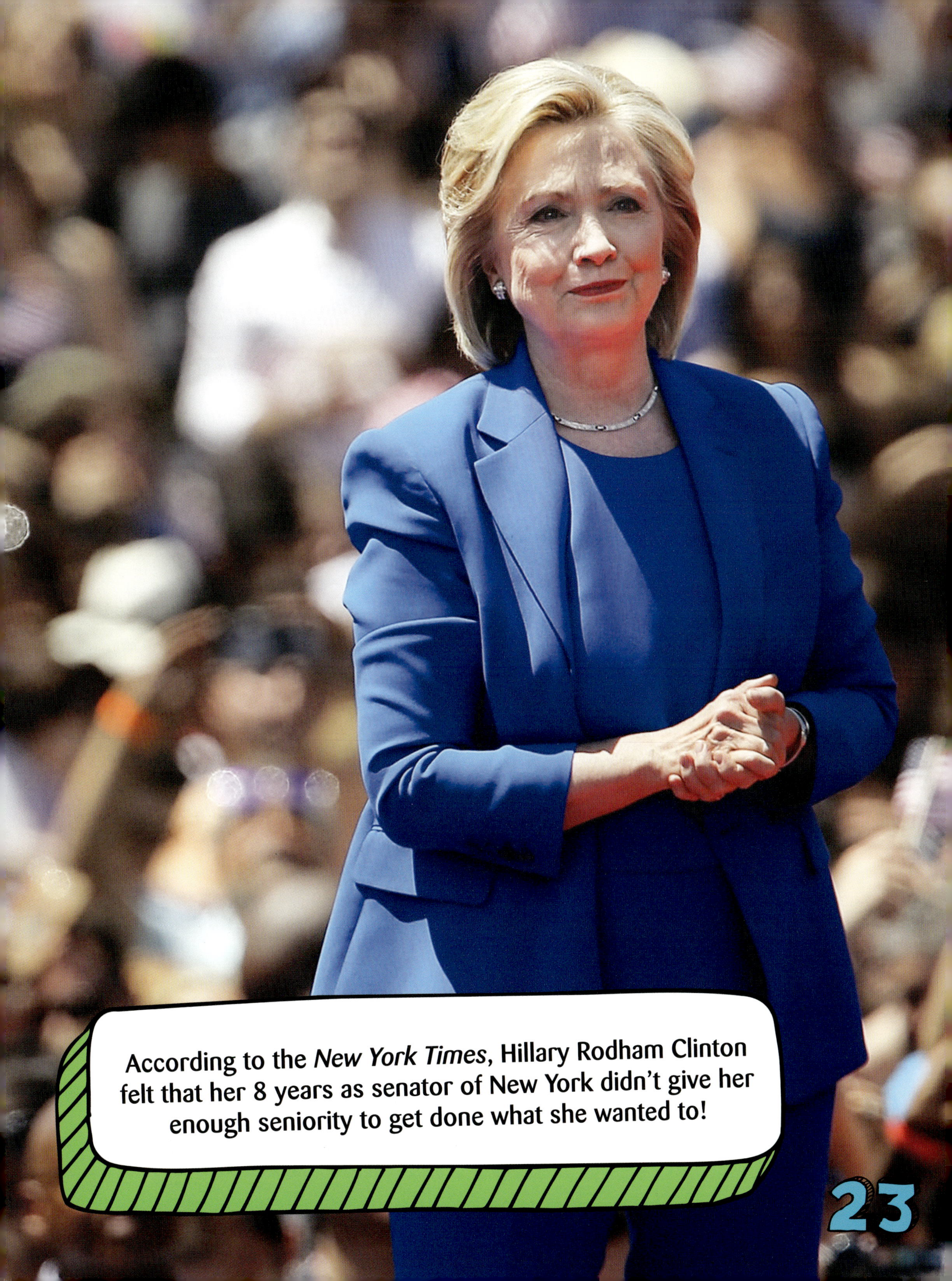

According to the *New York Times*, Hillary Rodham Clinton felt that her 8 years as senator of New York didn't give her enough seniority to get done what she wanted to!

Leading the Senate

Senate leadership is often based on seniority as well. Each political party chooses a leader. The leader of the party who has the largest number of senators is called the Senate majority leader. The leader of the party with the smaller number of senators is called the Senate minority leader. The senators chosen for these positions generally have a lot of experience and influence.

Top Spots

The vice president is the president of the Senate, but only casts a vote when there's a tie vote in the Senate. When the vice president isn't present, the longest-serving senator from the majority party **presides** over the Senate. He or she is called the president pro tempore.

Those chosen as Senate majority and minority leader have a say in what senators from their party sit on which committees. The Senate majority leader makes even more important decisions: He or she decides what bills come to the Senate floor when.

US Senator Harry Reid from Nevada served as Senate majority leader from 2007 to 2015.

Would You Run for Senate?

A senator's job has a lot of long, tiring days. However, senators have a real effect on US laws, presidential appointees, and the lives of the citizens in their states. Does this interest you as a job?

If you're already running a club or trying to be elected to student council, you're on the right track! Working to build your leadership skills throughout your time in school will help you once you're old enough to run for Senate. That's not the only activity you can do to learn useful skills. Being a member of a sports team teaches you how to cooperate with others, for example.

What Makes a Good Senator?

Good senators share many qualities. They're willing to work hard and stand up for what they believe in. A senator can earn a good reputation by keeping promises and helping other senators with their agenda. The ability to remain positive, energetic, and focused is also helpful with the long hours senators work.

Speaking to newspaper and TV reporters is part of senators' work. That includes holding press conferences to spread the word about their agenda.

Schoolwork is very important to a future politician. Study hard in your social studies classes, especially when learning how the US government works. Paying close attention in writing classes may help you write a great campaign speech someday, too! Good grades in general are likely needed to become a senator. Most senators attend college, and many earn a master's degree or higher! Degrees in political science or law are particularly helpful.

Social Senators

Senators often have to attend parties, fundraisers, and other events. They need to be comfortable talking to groups of people, both large and small. Events are often in the evening after a senator has worked a full day, and it can be tiring to socialize. However, it may help a senator's future campaign!

Senator Tom Carper and Martha Carper

What else can you do to build your **résumé**?

- Volunteer in your community.
- Keep up-to-date on current news events.
- Work on a local political campaign.
- Take a public-speaking class.

Senators stand up for what they believe in. What's important to you about the future of the United States?

GLOSSARY

administrator: someone whose job is to run a school or company

agenda: a list of things to get done or talk about

constituency: the people who live and vote in an area

debate: an argument or public discussion

influence: the exercise of power

legislature: a lawmaking body

lobbyist: someone who works to influence government decisions about an issue or industry

naturalize: to allow someone born in a different country to become a citizen

preside: to lead or to be in a position of authority

primary: an election at which members of the same political party run against one another for the opportunity to run in a major election

résumé: a list of accomplishments often given when applying for a job

seniority: the status gained by the length of time of continuous service in a position

volunteer: a person who works without being paid

FOR MORE INFORMATION

BOOKS

Cane, Ella. *The U.S. Senate.* North Mankato, MN: Capstone Press, 2014.

Nagelhout, Ryan. *Standing in a Senator's Shoes.* New York, NY: Cavendish Square Publishing, 2016.

Steinkraus, Kyla. *How a Bill Becomes a Law.* Vero Beach, FL: Rourke Educational Media, 2015.

WEBSITES

Congress for Kids: Legislative Branch
www.congressforkids.net/Legislativebranch_index.htm
Read all about the governmental bodies that make US laws.

How Laws Are Made
kids.clerk.house.gov/grade-school/lesson.html?intID=17
Find out the steps behind lawmaking.

Publisher's note to educators and parents: Our editors have carefully reviewed these websites to ensure that they are suitable for students. Many websites change frequently, however, and we cannot guarantee that a site's future contents will continue to meet our high standards of quality and educational value. Be advised that students should be closely supervised whenever they access the Internet.

INDEX